Contents

Just Kidding!

Jordan Brown

SCHOLASTIC INC.
New York   Toronto   London   Auckland   Sydney
Mexico City   New Delhi   Hong Kong

For my new son.
May your life be filled with love and laughter.

Thanks to Tina Posner and Allen Mogol
for their great suggestions.

Cover illustration and interior illustrations
by Brad Hamann

Copyright © 2001 by Scholastic Inc.
All rights reserved. Published by Scholastic Inc.
Printed in the U.S.A.

ISBN 0-439-31282-5

SCHOLASTIC, READ 180, and associated logos and designs are
trademarks and/or registered trademarks of Scholastic Inc.
LEXILE is a trademark of MetaMetrics, Inc.

5   6   7   8   9   10   23   10

1 If It's Laughter You're After

Who's the funniest person you know?

I don't mean some comedian on TV or in the movies. I'm talking about someone in your real life who can crack you up no matter what.

The funniest person in my life is Cosmo Cruz. Laugh for laugh, he's simply the best. Everyone at our middle school agrees. Cosmo is not your typical class clown either. He doesn't go for the easy yuks. You won't see him making gross noises with his armpits. Any bozo can do that.

No, Cosmo's a pro. He loves to make people laugh when they least expect it. He says his day isn't complete if he hasn't made milk squirt out someone's nose.

Speaking of noses, I remember the day that

Cosmo had a big red pimple on his. We're talking a major zit—the size of a cherry. Most kids would have skipped school. But not Cosmo!

That morning, he strolled into homeroom as usual. Everyone stared at him, pointed at his face, and laughed. They weren't being mean. With a thick red marker, Cosmo had drawn an arrow on his cheek – pointing right at his zit. Next to the arrow, he wrote: PANIC BUTTON.

It is not surprising that Cosmo is a comic genius. After all, he's my twin brother.

I'm Lucy Cruz. I was born two minutes ahead of him. I like to call him my "younger brother." He gets annoyed when I say that. But I can't help it. Like having brown eyes and a killer smile, making jokes is part of being in the Cruz family.

Over to you, bro.

How does Lucy feel about her brother, Cosmo?

2 I Love Lucy, Too

Hey, there. Cosmo here. Wow, that was some introduction, Lucy. What a build up. Really, it was too much. How can I live up to all that? I think the funny part of my brain is choking. I can't handle the pressure. Aaaaaaaagggggghhhh!

Just kidding. I don't mean to brag, but being funny has always come easy to me. When Lucy and I were little kids, I used to make her giggle all the time by sticking French fries in my ears. Sure, my ears got greasy, but it was worth it.

Humor is a big deal in our family. In fact, even our names are funny. I was named after a character on the old television show *Seinfeld*. My parents loved the character Kramer. Of course, Kramer was his last name. As true fans, my parents knew Kramer's first name— Cosmo. Weird as it sounds, I think I may have gotten more than my name from this character. I think I got his crazy hair, too. Sometimes when I wake up, it looks like a someone held a salsa dancing contest on my head.

My "older sister," Lucy, is named after Lucille Ball, the star of *I Love Lucy*. Every now and then, we catch reruns of that old show on cable. They're hilarious.

By the way, my sister is really funny, too. Once a week, she writes a "Top Three" list and posts it in the lunchroom. Last week, she wrote the "Top Three Lamest Excuses for Not Turning in Your Homework." Number three: I was abducted by space aliens. Number two: I was out fighting crime in my ballet tights. Number one: I accidentally used a pen that had invisible ink!

She also comes up with these great nicknames for our teachers. My personal favorite is the one she invented for Ms. Grippo, our librarian. Ms. Grippo is incredibly grouchy.

She's always yelling. What's up with that? Anyway, Lucy named her Ms. Get-a-grip-o. Of course, that's just our little secret.

Lucy and I are each other's biggest fans. She thinks I'm hilarious. I think she's hilarious. And it makes you want to barf, right? Well, you should have seen us last March. That was when we were competing in a contest called Operation Gag. Things were a little less than friendly around here. We both wanted to win that contest—bad.

What's Operation Gag? What contest? Take it easy. We're getting to it.

Why do you think Cosmo and Lucy are so close?

3

No Yuck At All

It all began one day in the school cafeteria. Cosmo and I noticed this new kid sitting by himself at one of the lunch tables. He had a magazine in front of him. But he was looking kind of lost. So we decided to go over there and welcome him with the old Cruz charm.

"How's it going, man?" Cosmo said, holding his hand out for a shake. "I'm Cosmo. And this is my twin, Lucy. I don't think we've met yet. Are you new?"

The kid answered, "Yeah. My name is Will Nayaki. I just moved here."

"Well, we'd be happy to show you the ropes, dude" my bro offered.

"Thanks," Will said.

Then Cosmo pointed to the flagpole outside the window. "Look, ropes. And I'm sure there are some more in the gym."

I thought Will might crackle a small grin. But, no, he didn't even groan. He just said, "Ooookay." Then he went back to eating his hamburger.

"Yeah, that was lame," Cosmo admitted.

Will started sipping his milk. That's when Cosmo got this gleam in his eye. He said, "Hey, know what you get when you cross a cheetah with a hamburger? Fast food!"

I chuckled at Cosmo's joke. Will didn't even smile. He just sort of nodded in Cosmo's direction. Cosmo was breaking out into a sweat. He'd never bombed like this before.

Cosmo started to pick up a French fry off his tray. I could tell he was going to stick it in his ear. I quickly shook my head at Cosmo. Hey, we're not five anymore! Plus, there was no way that Will would laugh at that.

Anyway, I decided to change the subject. I said, "Listen, Will, I'm vice president of the drama club. We are holding auditions today for

the spring play. Want to come?"

"No, thanks," said Will. "I'm trying out for the swim team."

"Good luck. I mean, break a fin," I said.

He just stared into space.

I continued, "Get it? Break a leg. Break a fin."

"Ooookay," he said flatly.

Wow, Cosmo and I both struck out completely. That never happens.

How would you have responded to Cosmo and Lucy's jokes?

4 The Big Idea

That night at home, Lucy and I were watching the comedy channel, eating popcorn, and drinking our favorite chocolate banana milkshakes. During a commercial, we started talking about Will.

"I can't figure out why he didn't laugh at any of our jokes," I said. "All he said was, 'Ooookay...,'" I imitated Will's voice. "But just wait till tomorrow." I rubbed my hands together and spoke in a voice like Dr. Evil from the Austin Powers movies. "His laughter will be MINE!!!" I then did this wild laugh.

Then Lucy said, "Listen, I'll bet I can make Will laugh before you can." Then, imitating Dr. Evil, she said, "I think his laughter will be MINE!!!" She did the laugh, too.

"Oh, really," I said smugly. "I accept your challenge."

"A contest it is," said Lucy.

"Well, then what will I win?" I said.

"What will *you* win? Nada. Zip. Zero. *I'm* the one who's going to win," said Lucy.

I suggested, "How's this? The winner gets a free ride in the kitchen. The loser does the dishes for a month."

"Nah, that's boring," Lucy said. "How about the loser takes out the trash for a month."

"No, that wouldn't be fair. I don't want you to have carry those smelly bags," I joshed.

"I'm not going to lose," Lucy insisted. "I've got this really funny gag—"

"Gag...gag...that's it!" I held up my milkshake and said, "The winner gets to mix up a really gross milkshake. And the loser has to drink it. Now *that's* a gag!"

"In front of everyone at school!" Lucy added.

"You're on!" I said. "Operation Gag begins tomorrow."

We sealed the bet by clinking our milkshake glasses.

"I hope you like liver and garlic in your milkshakes," Lucy said.

She didn't scare me.

How would you make Will laugh?

5 Let the Gags Begin

The next morning, I started writing a recipe for Cosmo's milkshake. So far, I had the following ingredients: tuna fish, chocolate syrup, baloney, garlic, and peppermint.

Cosmo darted into the kitchen and glanced over my shoulder.

"Don't forget the liver!" he said. "I can't wait to take a picture of your face when you get a taste of that shake."

"Don't you wish!" I said. "And just for that I'm adding tomatoes to my list. I know how much you love them, bro."

"Not tomatoes! You know those evil red things and I just don't get along."

It was true. My brother hates tomatoes

more than anything.

I looked at the clock. The bus would be at the corner in five minutes.

"We better get out of here," I said.

Cosmo and I put on our coats, gloves, and scarves, and headed toward the front door.

"Wait a second. I forgot something," I said. I ran over to the kitchen cabinet and stuffed a jar of peanut butter into my backpack.

We made it to the bus just in time.

Cosmo was first to spot Will in the hallway at school. Quickly, Cosmo reached into his locker. He pulled out his math book and balanced it on his head. Then he added his science book and social studies book, followed by three overdue library books. Cosmo paraded down the hallway balancing all six books on his head.

Cosmo walked over to Will and said "As you can see, I have a lot on my mind today." Will stared at all the books and smiled.

"That's pretty cool," Will said. "Where'd you learn to do that?"

Before Cosmo could answer, I walked up and said, "Most people don't know that our

family sold Cosmo to the circus. But, they wanted a refund, so we had to take him back."

Will was a tough one. I couldn't get him to crack a smile.

Then Cosmo said, "Hey, Will, check this out." He lifted his right leg into the air. He stuck his arms out the side for balance. A group of kids watched Cosmo and giggled.

Cosmo leaned next to Will and whispered, "It drives the babes wild."

My brother didn't realize that I overheard.

"Oh, yeah," I said. "I have always found it hard to resist a guy with flat head."

Cosmo made a face at me, then asked Will, "You're in social studies with us, right?"

"That's right." Will may not laugh much, but he had a super smile. It faded as he turned around to look at Cosmo.

"Ahhhhh…..Ahhhhhhh….Ahhhh….."

Cosmo was doing his super sneeze. I have to admit that I was worried. Cosmo could get anyone to laugh with this gag.

"Ahhhhh….Ahhhhhhh…Ahhhh!" Cosmo continued. His body swayed, but the books stayed in place. "Chooooo!" Cosmo finished his sneeze. All the books crashed to the ground. The students in the hallway cracked up.

Will bent down to help pick up the books. His face was completely straight.

"Ooookay," Will said.

I whispered to Cosmo, "I guess Operation Gag is still on." Now it was my turn.

How do you think Will feels about Cosmo?

6 You Said a Mouthful

In social studies class, I sat next to Will. For the last two weeks, our class had been doing oral reports about American heroes. Lucy was giving her report on George Washington Carver today.

"George Washington Carver was born in Missouri in 1864," Lucy began. "He taught himself so much about plants that he got the nickname 'the Plant Doctor.'"

Lucy spoke for about five more minutes, talking about Carver's life and his accomplishments.

"In my opinion George Washington Carver's greatest invention was peanut butter," she said to end her report.

Smiling sweetly, Lucy scooped a HUGE amount of peanut butter into her mouth.

Then she asked, "Does anybody have any questions?" But it sounded like, "La globby doby ga nabby gwazzoo?" The class burst out laughing. Well, everyone laughed except one person—Will.

After Lucy took her seat, I passed her a note.

NICE TRY. BUT IF YOU WANT TO SEE ME WIN THE CONTEST, COME TO THE POOL AT 4:00.

How do you think the teacher felt about Lucy's joke?

7 A Real Bird Brain

I got to the pool at 4:00. Oddly enough, there was no sign of Cosmo.

I sat for a while and watched the team do some laps. The chlorine from the pool was burning my eyes. And I was getting bored. Then came diving practice. Will walked toward the ladder. Suddenly, I saw something out of the corner of my eye.

A door from the boy's locker room opened and Cosmo walked into the pool area. My jaw dropped. Cosmo was wearing a suit and tie. Well, he was sort of wearing it. The suit was two years old and barely fit. His wrists and ankles were sticking out. The tie was too short, and the jacket buttons were popping. His normally wild hair was slicked back. His dress shoes make a click-click-click sound as he walked briskly toward the pool.

As Will climbed the ladder, he noticed Cosmo and waved. My brother gave him the thumbs-up sign.

Will was standing on the diving board, concentrating. I looked over at Cosmo, waiting for him to do something silly. But Cosmo just stood there and smiled. Will did a back flip. He entered the water with barely a splash.

Cosmo and I walked over to talk to Will.

"Very impressive, Will," I said.

"Good job, man. I may be able to balance books on my head, but what you did was truly amazing. Way to go!" said Cosmo.

"Thanks," Will said. He seemed surprised to see us there.

"Listen," Cosmo said. "A friend of mine would like to meet you, but he's hiding. He's kind of a chicken. I'll have to go get him."

Before Will could say anything, my brother headed back to the locker room. When he came out, he had a large blow-up chicken under his arm.

Then Cosmo did a little dance with the blow-up chicken. At one point he held the chicken over his head and twirled himself around and around.

I looked over at Will. He had no expression on his face. What was this guy made of?

"Woooooooah!" said Cosmo.

I looked back over at my brother. One minute he was dancing on the edge of the pool. The next, he was splashing wildly in the water making chicken noises.

I tried not to laugh, but it was impossible. I had tears in my eyes, and it wasn't from the chlorine. I walked over to Will ready to admit defeat. I said, "My brother is too funny, right?"

Will's expression looked almost serious. "Ooookay, Lucy, if you say so."

Cosmo tossed the chicken out of the pool, then climbed out himself. He was completely soaked. He looked over at me eagerly.

I shook my head "no." Then I pointed at him and pretended to drink a big glass. I stuck my tongue out to show that it tasted foul.

Speaking of "foul," Cosmo tried one last desperate move. On the ground, he pretended to save the chicken's life with mouth-to-beak resuscitation.

"Call the time, Lucy," said Cosmo, finally, imitating the doctors on TV when they lose a patient.

Will just gave a pleasant smile. He said, "Thanks again for coming to practice. "

"No problem," said Cosmo.

"Too bad about your chicken, Cosmo," Will said.

Cosmo and I shot each other a look. Was it possible? Was Will making a joke? Maybe it wasn't as hopeless as we thought.

What has Will done to give Cosmo and Lucy some hope?

8 Now That's No Joke

A loud banging noise over my head Saturday morning woke me out of a deep sleep.

I hopped out of bed, put on my slippers, and walked downstairs. My hair looked like I had combed it with an electric mixer.

Lucy was still asleep. But Mom was in the kitchen reading the newspaper and drinking a cup of tea.

"What's that noise?" I asked, pointing upward.

"Your father is trying to fix the roof," Mom said. "Some shingles broke off during the storm last week."

"Is he insane?" I asked. "It's like 10 degrees out. He'll get frostbite or something." I grabbed a handful of dry cereal straight from the box.

"You know your father. Once he sets his mind on something, that's it," said Mom.

I ran upstairs and got dressed. Then I walked out the front door to see how he was doing. I saw a tall ladder stretching from our front lawn to the roof just above my room.

"Hey, Dad. Thanks for the wake up call!" I shouted sarcastically.

"Sorry, Cosmo. I thought you'd be up."

"It's only 8:30," I said.

My father pounded a nail.

"I'm almost done," he said. I watched him pound a few more nails in. He called out, "Done!"

My father stood up and held onto our chimney.

"Dad, be careful!" As soon as the words left my mouth, I realized my mistake. Sometimes my father acts like a two-year-old. If you tell him not to do something, that's exactly what he does.

He leaned against the chimney and took a deep breath. Then he stretched his arms out, looking like an airplane. He looked upward and shouted, "I'm king of the world!!"

"Would you please come down," I begged. "You're making me nervous."

"Just a second," he said.

I actually wasn't that worried. My dad has an amazing sense of balance. He was the one who taught me how to clown around with all those books balanced on my head.

"Could you hold the ladder steady for me?" he asked.

He put his hammer in his belt and slowly climbed down. Every few seconds, he pretended to slip and said, "Whoooaa!" My heart would suddenly stop until I heard my dad chuckle and say, "Phew, that was a close one."

"Dad! Stop clowning around!"

Then he let out a "Yaaaaagghh!" And he fell on the ground.

I ran over to him.

"Dad, Dad are you okay? Stop kidding!"

His eyes were shut and his mouth was open. His right leg was twisted in a strange position. I patted his face. "Dad, can you hear me?"

No reaction. He was out cold.

Lucy flew out the front door. "What happened? I heard something—" she said. Then she saw my father lying in the snow.

"Mom!!!" We both called. "Mooooom!"

Suddenly Operation Gag didn't seem very important.

What happened to Cosmo and Lucy's dad?

9

Broken Funny Bones

My mom called "911" and an ambulance arrived in less than five minutes. The EMS people carried my dad into the ambulance on a stretcher. My mom, Cosmo, and I all rode in the back with him.

The EMS person in back with us said to me, "He's in shock. And it looks like his leg is broken. We'll know for sure when we get to the hospital."

The siren blared as we raced down Main Street. I put my hand on Cosmo's shoulder. He was a wreck. He hadn't stopped crying for 20 minutes.

"What happened? Where am I?" My dad

was awake but still seemed out of it.

"DAD!!!" Cosmo and I shouted. At the same moment, my mom cried, "Danny!!!"

"You fell off that ladder, Dad," Cosmo said. "That's right…," my Dad said weakly.

A few seconds later, my dad was out again.

Later that night, we were sitting in my dad's room at the hospital. His leg was wrapped in a cast and raised in the air with a pulley.

Mom had taken Cosmo to the cafeteria to get some dinner. He hadn't eaten all day. I kept Dad company and did crossword puzzles with him.

The nurse brought in his dinner. I looked down at the tray.

"Peas in gravy! Gross!" Dad said.

There was mystery meat in there, too. Yuck. Good thing he got some Jell-O and a vanilla shake in a can.

Shakes! It hit me. I hadn't thought of Operation Gag once all day. While my dad ate, I told him about the contest. I acted out the stories about the peanut butter and the chicken in the pool.

"It only hurts when I laugh," my dad said.

I was so glad to hear my dad laugh again.

"You'd better let your dad get some rest," the nurse said, but she was laughing too.

Before my dad dozed off, I asked him if he had any ideas about how I could make Will laugh. My dad said, "Oh no. I'm not getting in the middle of Operation Gag." Then he rolled over and began snoring.

Why was Lucy happy to hear her father laugh?

10 Falling Apart At the Seams

On Monday, Lucy and I agreed to continue Operation Gag. There was one more week left in March. We agreed that if neither one of us could get Will to laugh by the end of the month, we'd call it a tie. A tie meant that we'd both have to drink the "muck-shake." That's what we started calling it. By this time, the list of gross ingredients was pretty long. They now included: spinach, pickle juice, sardines, and beef gravy.

That morning I was standing by my locker when I saw Will. He asked how my weekend was, and I told him about my father's accident. He looked worried. But he was glad to hear that my father was getting better.

I pulled my math book out of my locker.

Will and I had math together second period.

I noticed Lucy way at the end of the hallway. "Wait right here, Will. I have to ask Lucy a quick question. Lucy, wait up!"

As I ran toward her, Will shouted, "Cosmo! Your sweater!"

I was wearing a really ugly purple and yellow sweater that one of my cousins had grown out of. Secretly, I had hooked a loop of yarn on my locker. As a ran, the sweater started to unravel. Will kept calling out for me to stop, but I kept running.

"I can't hear you," I called back to Will. I pretended I had no idea that my sweater was coming apart.

About halfway to Lucy, I turned around and saw a river of yarn behind me. I pretended to be horrified. Then I went back to gather up the purple and yellow mess. But on the way I "accidentally" wrapped the yarn around as many students as possible. Laughter filled the hallway. Lucy kept a close watch on Will. He didn't even chuckle. When I had finally gathered all the yarn, I walked back to my

locker.

"I was going to ask you to help me carry my science project," Lucy shouted to me, "but I can see you're all tied up."

"C'mon, Cosmo, we'd better go," Will said to me. And we walked down the hallway to class. I couldn't believe it. The guy was made of stone. Either that, or I really was losing my touch.

How do you think this contest will end?

11 Gag-o-licious

Over the next few days, Cosmo and I each made last ditch efforts to get Will to laugh. But we got nowhere fast.

By then, everyone was whispering about Operation Gag. They couldn't wait to see who would win. They kept it a secret, but every time Cosmo or I did something silly, they quickly checked Will's reaction.

Finally, time ran out. Cosmo and I both had to admit defeat. Tomorrow we'd have to face the consequences.

On the last day of the contest, I posted a note in the cafeteria. It said: Top 3 Ways to Enjoy a Muck-shake. Number three: Hold your nose. Number two: Have your taste buds amputated. Number one: Watch your brother have to drink it too!

It was time for the moment of truth. Cosmo and I headed to the cafeteria with our bags. There were probably a hundred kids watching us. The air was filled with excitement. Will was there, too.

While Cosmo and I usually love attention, today was different. I pulled a blender out of one of the bags. Cosmo pulled two big blue glasses out of another.

"Well, this is it," Cosmo said. "I said I would win. But now it's looks like I'll have to eat my words."

"Drink them, you mean," I said. Then I opened a can of sardines, and took a bottle of chocolate sauce out.

"Let's begin," Cosmo announced. The room quieted down. Quiet giggles were heard as we added the ingredients.

"Tuna fish," I said as dumping it in the blender.

"Lima beans," he said.

"Chopped tomatoes," I said with an evil

smile. Cosmo stuck his tongue out.

We went on filling the blender with disgusting ingredients until it was almost full.

I held the top on the blender with both hands.

"Stand back, everyone. This isn't going to be pretty," Cosmo warned. He flipped the switch.

WWWRRRRRRRRRRRRRRRRR!

The "muck-shake" swirled around. It was a brownish gray with different colored pieces floating in it. It was as thick as mud.

"I hope it's fat-free," Cosmo said. "I'm on a diet, you know."

I clinked glasses with my brother. We were ready.

Suddenly Will stepped forward. He walked up to where we were standing. "I'd like to say…How shall I put it…?"

He stood there silent for a full minute. Then he said, "Gotcha!"

Will threw back his head and burst out laughing. Finally, he found *something* funny. But what?

"Ha Ha Ha Ha Ha Ha Ha Ha Ha Ha Ha
Ha Ha Ha Ha Ha Ha Ha Ha Ha Ha Ha

Ha Ha Ha Ha Ha Ha Ha Ha Ha Ha Ha
Ha Ha Ha Ha Ha Ha Ha Ha Ha Ha Ha
Ha Ha Ha Ha Ha Ha Ha Ha Ha Ha Ha!"

Tears were rolling down Will's checks. I thought he would never stop.

Gasping and choking, Will said, "Let me explain; at my old school I was the funny guy. Then, the first day I came here, I kept hearing about how hilarious you two are. Cosmo this, Lucy that. So, I decided to play a little joke on you. I forced myself not to laugh at any of your jokes." Will laughed some more. "Look, you guys don't have to drink that muck-shake. The contest was fixed from the start. Neither of you had a chance!"

Cosmo and I were speechless. No one had ever played a joke on us before. Cosmo and I looked at each other and smiled. At the same time, we both poured our muck-shakes over Will's head.

Will laughed even harder and longer. Then he hugged us both. Yuck!

Afterward, we borrowed a mop and some sponges from the kitchen. It took us about an

hour to clean up the mess.

That smell will haunt me forever.

What joke did Will play on Cosmo and Lucy?

12 It's All in a Name

The following Saturday, my dad came home from the hospital. He was still walking on crutches, but he was doing great. Mom, Lucy, and I put together a celebration for him. (Lucy suggested calling it a "cast party.")

We invited Will to the party. In his honor, we served milkshakes. But these milkshakes were chocolate and banana. Our parents made us tell the story again. No matter how many times we told it, our parents loved hearing about Operation Gag.

Will put his hand on my shoulder and said, "I've got to ask you a question. Please don't take this the wrong way. How did you get a weird name like Cosmo?"

I explained that Lucy and I were named after famous funny people—Lucille Ball and Cosmo Kramer from *Seinfeld*.

"You're not going to believe this, but I was named after a comedian, too. Will Smith!"

"That's incredible," Lucy said.

"I want to make a toast," I said, holding my milkshake glass in the air. Lucy and Will did the same. "Here's to the funniest people in the world!" Just as Lucy and Will were blushing, I added, "Oh, and both of you, too."

On cue, Lucy and Will poured their milkshakes on my head.

It was the start of a beautiful friendship.

What do Will, Lucy and Cosmo all have in common?